Last Stories of Polly and the Wolf

by the same author

CLEVER POLLY AND THE STUPID WOLF
ADVENTURES OF POLLY AND THE WOLF
(POLLY AND THE WOLF AGAIN in Puffin)
TALES OF POLLY AND THE HUNGRY WOLF
PUSS AND CAT
ROBIN
KATE AND THE ISLAND
THE STORY OF THE TERRIBLE SCAR
THE CATCHPOLE STORY
THE PAINTER AND THE FISH
UNDERGROUND CONSPIRACY
MARIANNE DREAMS
MARIANNE AND MARK
COLD MARBLE
THE CASTLE BOY
VICKY
THE CHINESE EGG
RUFUS
THURSDAY
THE BOY AND THE SWAN (André Deutsch)

Last Stories of Polly and the Wolf

Catherine Storr

Illustrated by
Jill Bennett

faber and faber
LONDON · BOSTON

First published in 1990
by Faber and Faber Limited
3 Queen Square London WC1N 3AU

Photoset by Parker Typesetting Service Leicester
Printed in England by
Clays Ltd St Ives plc

A CIP record for this book is available from the British Library

ISBN 0-571-14308-3

CONTENTS

THE WOLF AT SCHOOL

Polly was on her way to school one morning, when she found the wolf trotting beside her. There were a great many other people around, so she was not particularly frightened, but she was curious.

'Where are you going, Wolf?' she asked.

'I'm going to school,' the wolf replied.

'My school?' Polly said.

'Of course, your school. Isn't it the best round here?' the wolf asked.

'Much the best. But Wolf . . . if you're thinking you'll be able to get to eat me in school, you'll be disappointed. There are always crowds of us all together. If you tried to eat me, you'd get caught and probably shot. Or something.'

The wolf wasn't listening. 'Crowds? Of plump little girls? Of good, juicy little boys? Like this lot here?' he asked, looking round at the pavement covered with children hurrying towards the school gates.

'You won't have a chance to eat any of them,' Polly said, answering what she knew was in the wolf's mind.

'Hm. Pity. But I don't know why you are always thinking about food. That's not what I am going to school for. My mind is on higher things,' the wolf said virtuously.

'Higher than what?'

'Higher than my stomach. Brains, you stupid little girl. I am going to school to develop my brains. I am going to school so that I can become clever. Even cleverer than I am already,' the wolf added hastily.

'Who told you school would make you clever?' Polly asked.

'Read it in the paper. There was an advertisement. DO YOU WANT YOUR CHILD TO BE SMARTER THAN ANYONE ELSE'S? START EARLY LEARNING LESSONS NOW. I know you have lessons at school, and as I haven't got a child it seemed meant for me. I shall stay in your school until I can outsmart you, Miss Polly. Then, when I've eaten you up, and perhaps a dozen or so of these other children, I shan't need to learn any more and I shall leave.'

By now they had reached the school gates, and the other children were squeezing their way through. 'I don't think you can just walk in and join in the lessons without asking,' Polly said to the wolf, as they stood outside, left to the last.

'You must introduce me. Go on! If you're so clever, you can think of some way of getting me in. If you don't . . . Grrrrrr,' the wolf said, showing his teeth.

Polly looked round and saw that they were alone. 'All right. I'll try,' she said, and they went together across the playground to the cloakroom door.

'Good morning, Polly,' said Miss Wright, but when she saw Polly's companion, she said, quickly, 'You know we don't allow pets in the classroom. Your dog must go home. Immediately!'

'He's not a dog. He's a friend who's come to stay with us from abroad. To learn English,' Polly said quickly, while she whispered to the wolf, 'Get up on your hind legs and try to look like a friend from abroad,' Beside her she could hear the wolf growling. 'Dog! Pet! Never been so insulted in my life!'

'He's very large. Isn't he too old for this class?' Miss Wright asked.

'He's big for his age,' Polly said.

'He's very dark. And hairy.'

'He's foreign. He doesn't speak the language very well yet. If he could sit next to me, I could help him,' Polly said, thinking it would be better not to let the wolf sit next to Susie, who was the

plumpest girl in the room, or next to Freddie, who might tease him into behaviour unbecoming to a pupil in Miss Wright's class.

'Foreign? How interesting. What country does he come from? What are you, dear?' Miss Wright asked the wolf. Polly wondered if he had ever been addressed as 'dear' before. His answer was indistinct, and Miss Wright looked puzzled for a moment, then she said, 'Hungary! Well now! I don't think we've ever had a child from Hungary in our school before. We must all do our best to make you feel at home.'

'I'd feel at home quicker if I could have something to eat,' the wolf muttered.

'What's that, dear? I didn't quite catch what you said.'

'He says he's feeling the heat,' Polly said.

'Really? You could take off your coat, if you're feeling too warm, dear. Now let's all get out our exercise books, shall we, for our first lesson? Numbers!'

'Take off my coat? Doesn't she know it's my skin?' the wolf said, a little too loud.

'What was that you said?' Miss Wright inquired.

'He said his coat is quite thin,' Polly said out loud.

'And what is your friend's name?' Miss Wright asked.

'Wol—— Wolly,' Polly said, having had no time to think up anything better.

'We don't like nicknames in this class. I shall call him by his proper name, Walter. When you speak to me, Walter, you must call me Miss Wright. Do you understand?'

'I will not be called by a stupid name like Walter!' the wolf said, very loudly indeed.

'What did you say?' Miss Wright asked.

'He says he wants a drink of water,' Polly said.

'Then he'll have to wait until the lesson is finished. I can't have you all running in and out whenever you feel like it. Now, we really must get on with the lesson. Let's see who can add up quickly, shall we? Who can tell me what ten and ten make?' Miss Wright began. Sally put her hand up, ready with the answer, but before she could speak, the wolf said, 'Ten what?'

'Do you know the answer, Walter? Good . . . good boy. What is it then?'

'Ten what?' the wolf repeated.

'It doesn't matter what. It's just a number, dear. Ten anything,' Miss Wright said.

'Of course it matters what. Ten buns would be good. Ten little pigs would be better. Ten fat little girls like that one would be better still. Only I haven't got a freezer, they'd be difficult to store. I'll settle for the pigs,' the wolf said.

'I don't know what you're talking about, dear. Perhaps they do numbers differently in your country. So we won't worry about buns or pigs, will we? So what do ten and ten make?' Miss Wright repeated.

'Twenty,' Polly said quickly. Numbers was one of her best subjects.

'She didn't put her hand up! I was going to say twenty!' Sally complained.

'I'll give you another question, then. What is twenty-four divided by eight?'

Sally took a little time to think about this. But the wolf had heard one of his favourite words. 'Who ate it? What did they eat?' he asked.

'Walter, didn't you hear me tell you that you

must say "Miss Wright" when you speak to me? And I didn't see your hand go up, either,' Miss Wright said.

'Five,' Sally said.

'No, that's not right. Very well, Walter, you tell us. Twenty-four divided by eight.'

'Was it the ten little pigs?' the wolf said.

'I wasn't talking about pigs.'

'Did they eat the buns?' the wolf went on.

'Three,' Polly said, loudly, hoping that Miss Wright would not hear this remark.

'What is three supposed to mean? Oh! Yes. Eight into twenty-four. Quite right, Polly. Now, who can tell me what seven and six make?'

By the end of the numbers lesson, the wolf was confused, Miss Wright was cross and Polly was exhausted. 'I don't think that can have made you any cleverer,' she said as they put away their books and got ready for the play they were rehearsing for the end of term.

'I've never heard such nonsense! What use are numbers if they aren't fastened to something? You don't see five or three or a hundred just floating about in the air. If she'd said five sausages, or three apples or a hundred beans, I'd have understood what she was getting at. It could even have been interesting. Now what do we do? Isn't it time for school dinner yet?'

'Not nearly. Miss Wright's going to give us our

parts for the school play.'

'What's the play about? If it's about little Red Riding Hood, I could act the wolf. I bet I'd do it much better than any of these silly little creatures,' the wolf said hopefully.

'It isn't Red Riding Hood. It's Hansel and Gretel. There isn't a wolf in it, so I don't know if Miss Wright will let you have a part.'

'I know that story! They get lost in a wood, don't they? I'm sure there must have been a wolf in that wood. Woods in fairy stories always have wolves in them.'

'This one didn't. It had a witch who lived in a gingerbread house.'

'Why gingerbread? Nasty stuff. It makes my throat tickle.'

'To catch children who liked it. Then she cooked them and ate them.'

'That sounds like a good part. I shall be the witch.'

Polly thought this was unlikely. But when Miss Wright was distributing the parts, no one else, except a very small boy called Eric, wanted to act as a witch, and at last Miss Wright was forced to notice the large black paw which had been waved every time she offered the part to another child, who turned it down. 'You want to be the witch, Walter? Are you sure you can manage it? She doesn't have much to say, but . . .'

'She catches children to eat,' the wolf said.

'Don't worry, dear. You can be sure that our story has a happy ending, though of course I don't know how you may have heard it in Hungary.'

'Well, Wolf? Now you've had a whole day in my school, do you feel clever? Cleverer?' Polly asked as they came out of the gates at the end of the afternoon.

'Much cleverer. That story we were acting was an inspiration to me. In fact, I think I'll skip school tomorrow. I have some urgent business to attend to in another direction,' the wolf said, and, rather to Polly's relief, he hurried away.

It was a few days later, that, on her way home from school, Polly saw a curious construction standing shakily in the road near to her own home. It looked like a badly put together garden shed, made out of brown paper. Windows and doors were drawn on the paper. Some sticky tape fastened a candy bar on one wall. On another was written a message:

THIS HUSE IS MAD OF G JINJEBRED

Polly stood still to examine it. She had an idea that she knew who had put it there and who was likely to be inside it. While she was looking, the building shook violently, there was a tearing noise, and the paper of one of the windows burst open.

'Who's there?' said a voice.

'Me. Polly,' said Polly.

'A little girl? Lost in the wood?'

'I'm not lost and this isn't a wood. But I am a girl.'

'That's the important part. Have a candy bar,' said the voice.

'There's only one,' Polly said.

'It's for you.'

'I'm not sure . . .' Polly began, but before she could finish, the door of the house had been wrenched apart, and the wolf stood there, grinning at her horribly.

'Got you! I knew you'd never be able to resist a candy bar,' the wolf said.

'I haven't had it yet,' Polly pointed out.

'Hurry up, then. You eat that first, then I'll take you home with me and put you in my oven, like the witch did to Gretel. At last!' the wolf said, happily.

'I thought you didn't like gingerbread,' Polly said.

'Hate it. The gingerbread was for you, not me. What I'm looking forward to is a good roast dinner. Roast girl.'

'You haven't read your fairy stories carefully enough. Don't you know what happened to all

those children the witch roasted in her oven? They didn't turn into roast child, they turned into gingerbread,' Polly said.

'I don't believe you!' the wolf cried.

'Have a look at the play. I've got it here, because I'm learning my part,' Polly said, offering the book to the wolf, who looked quickly at the end, snarling with disappointment.

'It's a cheat! It can't be true! Do you mean to say, Polly, that if I roast you now, you're going to become a gingerbread girl? Like these pictures in the book?' the wolf asked.

'I should think so. It seems to be the rule when you catch someone with a house made of gingerbread and sweets,' Polly said.

'But I don't like gingerbread!' the wolf cried.

'I'm afraid that's all you're going to get,' Polly said.

'It isn't fair! That woman who taught us said the story ended happily! This isn't a happy ending!' the wolf moaned.

'I don't think she meant it would be happy for a wolf. Too bad. You'll have to think of something else, won't you? See you at school on Monday?' Polly called as she quickly made her escape. But somehow she didn't think the wolf would be coming back to school to make him clever enough to catch even cleverer Polly.

THE HIJACK

'Aha! Perfect! That's the modern way to catch your food. If I'm clever – and I am clever – I'll probably get several other children as well as Polly. Aha! Aha!' said the wolf, very much pleased with himself.

On Wednesday afternoons, a bus came to Polly's school to take Forms Two, Three and Four to the swimming baths, which were several miles away. There was always a rush to get on and to keep the best places – as far away as possible from Miss Wright, who was apt to be cross, and as near as possible to Miss Smith, who was cheerful and didn't mind a little noise. She would sometimes even join in the songs herself.

On this particular Wednesday Polly noticed that there was an extra passenger with them. There was Miss Wright, sitting at the back, and Miss Smith, sitting near the front. There was Mr Macklin the driver, whom they all knew quite well; and today there was someone else, wearing a duffle coat with a hood, and large dark glasses, sitting just behind Mr Macklin. Something about him seemed familiar, though Polly couldn't be quite sure what it was.

'Roll call! Everyone just say "Yes" when I call your name. And *stop talking* till I've finished,' Miss Smith shouted above the noise of thirty-five voices all speaking at once. She began.

'Toby Ames. Jenny Arlott. James Blagg . . .' down to 'Pearl Yates. Ivan Zada. Is that everyone?' she said, before she sat down.

'Please Miss, there's someone here who didn't have his name called,' Timmy said from near the front.

'Who is it? Will whoever didn't have his name called, please stand up,' Miss Smith said.

No one stood up. The children began whispering and pointing.

'Who is it? Be quiet, kids. Stand up, whoever it is,' Miss Smith said more loudly.

But still no one stood up.

'Please Miss, it's him,' Timmy said, and pointed at the figure in the duffle coat, just in front of him.

Miss Smith got up out of her seat and went over to the stranger. It was clear that he was not one of her pupils, so she was careful how she addressed him.

'Excuse me . . . I don't know if you realize that this is a private bus. Just for the pupils of Royston Road School. I think you must have got on by mistake.'

'No mistake. I meant to get on this bus,' the stranger said.

'But it's a private bus! And you don't belong to the school or the bus company. Do you?' Miss Smith asked.

'That's it. I belong to the bus company. I have to go along wherever the bus goes. In case something goes wrong,' the stranger said.

'You mean there's something wrong with it now? Then it shouldn't have been sent out this afternoon,' Miss Smith said.

'Accidents do happen. When this one does, I'll be there to look after everyone,' the stranger said.

Miss Smith noticed that the stranger was carrying a large black bag on his lap. 'Those are your tools, I suppose?' she said.

'What? Oh, this. Yes, that's my tools, all right,' the stranger said, and there was something about his smile that Miss Smith did not quite like. However, she went back to her seat, and when the driver said, 'All right, Miss? Do I get going?' she said, yes he should get going, and the bus lurched away from the school gates and spun cheerfully down the road.

But the traffic was dreadful. The journey was taking twice as long as it should have and the children grew impatient. They chattered and they sang; some of them started small fights, others began on the sandwiches and candy bars which their mothers had given them to refresh them after swimming. Miss Wright shouted at the noisier children and Miss Smith tried to amuse those in the seats near her. The driver swore softly to himself and sometimes leaned out of the window to swear more loudly at other drivers. The mechanic with the large black bag on his lap sat very still. Polly, who was sitting on the seat directly behind him, kept her eyes fixed on his back. She did not trust large persons who kept the hoods of their duffle coats over their heads when it wasn't cold, and wore dark glasses when it wasn't sunny. And who had such very large, sticking-out teeth.

They were in a busy High Street, with crowds of shoppers on the pavements and cars parked on both sides of the road, when there was a strange grinding noise in the engine, and the bus stopped abruptly.

'Driver! What are you stopping for?' Miss Wright demanded from her seat at the back.

'Very sorry, Miss. Something wrong. I'd best get out and have a look,' the driver said, and swung himself out of the cab. The children saw him open the bonnet and peer inside. Then he beckoned to the strange passenger.

'Come and have a look at this. And bring your tools,' he shouted.

'My tools?' asked the wolf (because of course it was the wolf), puzzled.

'Your tools in that bag,' Polly said, leaning forward.

'Ah, yes. This bag. But it isn't tools I have in this bag, it's something quite different. And now we've so conveniently stopped, I should inform you all that this is a hijack, and if you don't all do exactly what I tell you, I shall . . .'

'Wolf! You can't hijack the bus here,' Polly whispered.

'Why not? I've got a gun in this bag. I shall say I'm going to shoot anyone who stops me doing exactly what I want,' the wolf whispered back.

'Because of the crowd all around us. You don't think you can just start shooting any of us without those people out there seeing what you're doing, do you? They'd make sure you didn't get far with your hijack. People don't like seeing innocent little children being shot. And I don't think they'd like to see us being eaten, either,' Polly said.

'Innocent little children! Little fiends,' the wolf said, observing the bus full of squirming, screaming and scuffling pupils.

'Come on! You're the mechanic, why don't you help?' roared the driver.

'I really think you'd better go on pretending to be a mechanic just now,' Polly said to the wolf.

'But I don't know the first thing about cars or engines!' the wolf said.

'You'll have to pretend to. Because if anyone discovers who you really are, here in this road, you'll get pulled out of the bus and chased. Look, there's a woman with two dogs. I'm sure they'd love to be told to hunt you down,' Polly said.

The wolf climbed slowly out of the bus and

stood on the edge of the crowd of helpful passers-by, with their noses inside the bonnet. They were all discussing loudly and angrily what was wrong and what should be done about it. Luckily for him, it was not long before one of the clever men who was fiddling about round the engine, held up something, saying triumphantly, 'Wanted a bit of cleaning, that's all. Try her again!' he said to the driver, who got back into his cab, and put his foot on the accelerator. There was a buzz and a roar. The bus twitched and moved. The wolf gave one bound, managed to get his foot on the step and his paws on the bars of the door, and to pull himself inside. He sank down on to his seat and closed his eyes.

'Nearly missed the bus,' he murmured.

Polly thought hard. If the wolf meant to hijack them, if he really had a gun and several bombs in the black bag, she had got to try to be cleverer than him once again.

The bus turned a corner into a quiet road with trees down the middle. The wolf leant forward and said to the driver, 'Stop here.'

'This isn't the baths. What's wrong with you? Want to get out?' the driver said.

'Not yet. Just stop when I tell you to.'

'We're on the late side already, with the engine going phut on me like that. I can't just stop anywhere,' the driver said, accelerating.

The wolf put a paw into the bag he was carrying and pulled out a small gun.

'Do you know what this is?' he asked the driver.

'Can't look now, mate. You tell me,' the driver said.

'It's a gun. I'm holding it against the back of your head and unless you do what I say, I shall shoot you dead.'

'And if you shoot me, who's going to drive this bus and get the kids to their swimming on time?' the driver asked.

'No one need drive after I've shot you. And I'll deal with the children. So pull in to the side and stop now,' the wolf said.

'Suppose you just go back to your seat and stop playing silly games,' the driver said, undisturbed. He had been driving children for years and he knew the sort of tricks they got up to.

'That's not what you're supposed to say,' the wolf cried, exasperated.

'You tell me what I ought to be saying, then,' the driver invited.

'You ought to do what I tell you and stop the bus. Then I make everyone here lie down on the floor and be my hostages and then . . .' The wolf hesitated. He did not quite know how to explain that his next step would be to go home with two or three really succulent small boys or girls.

'Go ahead, then. Shoot,' said the driver cheerfully, not believing for a moment that this was serious.

'No, don't! If you kill the driver now, there'll be a horrible accident,' Polly cried. The wolf looked round at her.

'Come closer. I want to whisper. I won't bite,' he said. Polly leaned forward so that her ear was near the wolf's mouth. 'I can't shoot. It isn't a real gun,' he said.

'You mean it's a pretend? It looks real,' Polly said.

'It does, doesn't it? Real enough to take any-

one in. And anyway, in the stories I read, hijackers often don't have real guns, but everyone's so frightened, they do what they're told,' the wolf complained.

'Mr Macklin is a very brave man,' Polly said.

'But it's all right, because as well as a gun, I've got a bomb in this bag,' the wolf boasted.

'What do you mean to do with the bomb?' Polly asked.

'Blow up the bus, of course.'

'With you in it?'

'Of course not! How stupid can you get, Polly? First I shall get out, then the bomb will go off and kill everyone, except me.'

'Is it a real bomb?' Polly asked.

'Of course it's a real bomb. I made it. In my back garden. I've got a useful book that tells you how. All you need is . . . But I'm not going to tell you about that. I've labelled it, too. I'll show you,' the wolf said, and out of the bag he pulled a packet which he showed Polly.

'You see? Says "BOMB" on the wrapper,' he said.

'When will it go off, Wolf?'

'I told you. I shall leave it lying underneath one of the seats, and when it goes off I shall be safely outside. Not too near,' the wolf said, grinning at his own cleverness.

'So it's got a clock-thing inside it which tells it

when to go off without your having to touch it?'

The wolf thought about this. Then he said, 'I may decide to throw it instead.'

'When are you going to do it, Wolf?'

'In some quiet spot where we . . . where I shan't be interrupted. Now, keep quiet, Polly, while I explain to the driver what will happen if he doesn't stop when I tell him to,' the wolf said, impatient.

'What will happen if he doesn't stop?'

'Then I blow up the bus with my bomb.'

'But if he hasn't stopped, you'll still be in it. You'll get blown up, too.'

'I may be able to leap out at the last moment.'

'It won't be easy. This sort of bus has automatic doors. Only the driver can open them.'

'I shall tell him to do that. Then I jump out and hurl my bomb.'

'Wolf, just think. Mr Macklin knows that you won't want to be blown up too. As long as he keeps you here with us, you won't throw your bomb. So he isn't going to let you out,' Polly said. Sometimes she could hardly believe that even the wolf could be so stupid. Indeed he now looked really crestfallen.

'So what shall I do, Polly?' he asked.

'I think you'd better give up the whole idea,' Polly said as kindly as she could.

'Not throw my bomb at anything?'

'That's right. Not at anything.'

'Not hijack your bus?'

'Too difficult, Wolf.'

'You mean, I've come all this way, wearing these stupid clothes, and letting myself be deafened by your horrible little friends for the last half hour, and I'm not going to get anything out of it?' the wolf said, almost snarling.

'Not this time, Wolf.'

'That's what you always say. "Not this time!" "Try again another day." You never think of what it's like for me, a poor innocent, hungry wolf, who only asks for one or two juicy little boys or girls out of all this lot! No one would miss just one, Polly!' the wolf pleaded, looking round the crowded bus with sad, longing eyes.

'I'll tell you something to comfort you, Wolf. If you had managed to blow up this bus with all of us on it, you wouldn't have got anything you'd really want to eat. We'd all be in little tiny pieces, and we'd smell horribly of gunpowder, or whatever your bomb is made of. You really wouldn't like the taste at all, even if you managed to find any bits of person among the bits of bus,' Polly said.

'You're quite sure about that? Taste horrible?' the wolf asked.

'Disgusting.'

'You're not just saying that?'

'No. It's perfectly true.'

'It isn't fair! Every time I think up a really good way of catching you, something goes wrong! The stories in the newspapers about hijackings don't go like this. The driver does what he's told and the hijacker gets what he wants . . .'

'He doesn't always. He often gets sent to prison,' Polly interrupted.

'Even if he hasn't hurt anyone?'

'For having a gun. Or a bomb.'

'You mean you can get sent to prison for just having it? Even if you don't use it?'

'Yes, Wolf.'

'Even if you never meant to use it? Even if the whole thing was just a joke? A ha-ha joke? Like an April Fool?'

'Yes, Wolf.'

'Got you there at last. Everyone out!' Mr Macklin called, drawing up outside the entrance to the swimming baths and opening the doors.

'Don't push! Two at a time, and wait for me on the pavement,' Miss Wright called. The children took no notice, but hustled and squeezed to get out. The wolf sat gloomily in his seat and watched them. When the last person had left the bus and the crocodile of children was being led into the building by Miss Smith, Mr Macklin stood up and stretched.

'You'll have to get off here, mate. They'll be three-quarters of an hour or more, and I've got to lock the bus up while I go off for a cup of tea,' he said to the large person in the front seat.

'I'm going. But just tell me something,' the person said, picking up his black bag and moving towards the door.

'What's that, then? Best tea round here is at that caff up the road. Doughnuts are good too,' Mr Macklin said.

'I'm not interested in doughnuts. What I want to know is, what do you do to get someone to stop talking? Someone who argues about whatever you say you're going to do, so that you can't hear yourself think? And then you don't do whatever it was you thought of.'

'Don't listen to him. If it goes in one ear, let it go out the other. Don't stop it on the way, or it'll do terrible things to your brain. Think about something else, that's what I do. Food, mostly.'

'Food?' the wolf asked, interested.

'That's right. Food. I can always think about food if I'm getting bored.'

'But suppose they're the same thing? Food and the person talking?'

Mr Macklin looked hard at the wolf. 'How do you mean? Doughnuts don't talk, do they? Cups of tea don't talk. Sausages don't talk. Just go on thinking about what you want to eat, and then nothing anyone says is going to put you off your stroke.'

The wolf sighed loudly. 'You don't know Clever Polly,' he said, and, carrying his black bag, he walked sadly away.

THINKING IN THREES

'How did they do it? Goldilocks just walks in at the front door, without being asked, and if they'd remembered to bolt the bedroom window, they'd have got her. And I can't get Polly to my house without all the trouble in the world, and then I've never managed to keep her there,' the wolf said to himself, closing the book of fairy tales in which he had just read, for the twentieth time, the story of the Three Bears.

He thought deeply. Was it because they were bears, and not wolves? No. Goldilocks didn't know who lived in the house when she found it. She must have been hungry, that was why she'd gone into an empty house to eat their porridge. 'Easy-peasy. All I've go to do is to get some porridge,' the wolf thought. No sooner thought than done. He fetched his basket and set out for the shops.

'A pound of porridge,' he said to the man behind the counter.

'Sorry, sir, we don't sell porridge. Oats, sir,' the man said.

'Oats? I'm not a horse.'

'No, sir. I can see that you're not a horse. I didn't mean to be rude, sir. Oats is what porridge is made of. Very easy, it is. You just boil oats in water.'

'And that makes porridge?'

'Yes, sir. Instructions on the packet.'

The wolf took the packet and read the instructions. Making porridge did indeed seem easy. He bought two packets in case his efforts with the first did not prove successful, and went home very much pleased with himself. 'Aha, Miss Polly! I'll have you eating in my house very soon – and eaten soon, too,' he said to himself.

A day or two later, Polly was passing the end of the street where the wolf lived, when she smelled a really horrible smell. She looked along the road and saw a trickle of smoke coming out from under his front door. She ran as quickly as she could towards it, and arrived just as the door was thrown open, and a gush of smoke and a slightly singed wolf leapt out.

'Wolf! What's the matter? Is your house on fire?' Polly panted.

'What? Who? No, no. No cause for alarm. I just left something to cook for a little too long. Why, it's Polly!' the wolf said, wiping black paws on a black apron.

'Smells terrible. What were you cooking, Wolf?' Polly asked.

'Nothing particular. Porridge, that's all. Porridge,' the wolf said.

'I thought you didn't like porridge?'

'Hate it. Looks like putty, tastes like mud and feels . . . Ugh!' the wolf said.

'Then why . . .?'

'For a visitor. Which reminds me. I suppose you wouldn't care to come in and have a bite to eat, Polly?' the wolf asked, very sweetly.

'No, thank you, Wolf.'

'I could make the other packet.'

'Is that going to be porridge too?'

'How did you guess? I probably wouldn't burn it this time.'

'I'm really not hungry, thank you, Wolf.'

'Pity. Never mind. Another time,' the wolf said and watched Polly disappear up the road.

'I'm not going to make that disgusting stuff again. Chairs, that's what I need. Polly will come past my house, feeling very tired, and when she looks in and sees three chairs all empty and ready for her to sit on, she won't be able to resist coming in to try them out. I'll see what I can arrange to tempt her tomorrow,' the wolf said to himself.

It was not the next day, but a week later, that Polly was near the wolf's house again. She looked down the road and saw, not smoke this time, but a group of boys apparently reading something on his front door.

When she reached them, Polly saw a large sheet of paper fastened to the knocker, on which was written:

NOTICE

THERE ARE THREE CHAIRS IN THIS HOUSE

The boys were busy writing a message underneath.

So what? We've got four chairs and a put-U-up

The door opened suddenly, and the wolf bounced out.

'How dare you write on my door?' he shouted at the boys.

'Someone's been writing on it already,' one of the boys said.

'That doesn't mean you have any right to. Who wants to know that you've got a put-U-up?'

'Who wants to know you've got three chairs?' the boy answered.

'She does,' the wolf said, pointing with his head towards Polly.

'No, I don't.'

'Yes, you do. And one's too high, and one's too low, but the other's just right. Come in and try them,' the wolf said.

'I don't think I'd better,' Polly said.

'Yes, you'd better. It would be fun.'

'Not much. Not for me.'

'I'd enjoy having you,' the wolf said, and his long red tongue flicked out of his mouth for a minute. He laid a large black paw on Polly's shoulder and began to steer her in through the doorway.

'Why don't we all come in? Come on, boys,' Polly said, holding on to an arm she found near her.

'I asked you. I don't want all of them,' the wolf said, disgusted. But it was too late, the boys were already through the doorway and looking about the wolf's living room. There were indeed three chairs. The wolf had decided not to spend good money on buying anything new, but to adapt what he'd already got, to fit the story.

'Why is that chair on the table?' the smallest boy asked.

'To make it too high, of course. Stoopid!' the wolf replied.

'Stoopid yourself. Now no one can sit in it,' the boy said.

'Is this supposed to be a chair?' another boy asked. He was looking at what appeared to be a seat almost on the ground.

'That's the one that's too low. I chopped its legs off,' the wolf said, complacently.

'That's cruel. How would you like it if someone chopped your legs off?' the boy said.

'I'm not a chair. I'm a wo—— I mean, I don't need to be made any lower. I'm the proper height for a . . . for the sort of person I am,' the wolf said.

'This one's all right,' a third boy said, sitting in the only other chair.

'You shouldn't be sitting in it. Polly's supposed to do that,' the wolf complained.

'That's all right. I'm not tired. Thank you very much for showing us your interesting furniture, but I think it's time we went home to our teas,' Polly said, moving towards the door.

'No, wait! You haven't tried all the chairs yet and said this one's too high and this one's too low and this one's all right and then you break it,' the wolf said.

'If she doesn't want to break it, I will,' the third boy said, and before the wolf could stop him, he had got out of the chair, picked it up by one leg and brought it down on the corner of the table with a crash which sent splinters of wood flying round the room. The little chair lay sadly on the floor; it had lost three of its legs and its back was broken. 'Like that?' the boy asked.

'You wicked boy! You've broken my only good

chair! Go away and don't ever come back!' the wolf cried out. 'Not you, Polly. You stay here and I'll . . . I'll make some more porridge,' he said quickly.

'No, thank you, Wolf. I don't like porridge any more than you do.'

'But you haven't tried the beds!'

'You have three beds?' Polly asked. She knew

now which story the wolf had been reading lately.

'Well, nearly three,' the wolf said.

'And one's too soft and one's too hard, but the other one is just right? And I'm supposed to try them all and then go to sleep in the little one?'

'That's right! You'd make a good detective, Polly.'

'Thank you, Wolf. Would you tell me how you've managed about the beds? To make one too hard and the next too soft?'

The wolf smirked. It was not a pretty sight. 'It wasn't easy, I can tell you. First of all, I put a lot of stones and some firewood into the big bed, under the bottom sheet. That'll be hard enough, I thought, and I tried it, and it certainly was. Then for the middling-sized bed that's too soft, I thought there isn't anything softer than feathers, so I ripped open my pillows and I've covered my settee with feathers. It's so soft you can't hardly breathe. You'll see, Polly, when you come upstairs to try.'

'So now you haven't any pillows?' Polly asked.

'I sacrificed them for a good cause,' the wolf said.

'What about the last bed? The really comfortable one?'

The wolf looked embarrassed. 'I've had some trouble with that. To start with, I haven't got any more beds, and it didn't seem worth buying a brand new one just for such a short time. I tried putting two chairs together, but that wasn't a great success. I kept on falling down between them whenever I tried to stretch out. Then I made a sort of nest on the floor, but it was distinctly draughty. I thought perhaps you'd be able to advise me, Polly. After all, you're the person who's going to find it so comfortable. I did wonder if you could go to sleep in the dirty linen basket . . .'

'Certainly not! I'm not dirty linen.'

'Perhaps in the bath? It's quite dry, I don't use it very often.'

'Not the bath. Even if it hasn't been used for months.'

'You're being very difficult,' the wolf sighed.

'And Wolf, it's all very well to try to have to have three of everything, but there's one thing you haven't thought of that you can't have three of,' Polly said.

'No, there isn't. I had three bowls for the porridge, and three chairs – until that nasty child destroyed one. And I've nearly got three beds. There's the bottom drawer of my kitchen dresser, I could make that very cosy with a couple of dishcloths and an old towel. That would make three beds, wouldn't it?'

'But there's only one of you,' Polly said.

'Of course. I am unique!' the wolf said, proudly.

'There were three bears.'

The wolf looked at Polly. He hated to admit it, but it seemed to him that she was winning the argument again, just as she had always won all the arguments they'd ever had. At last he said, in a small voice, 'You mean, it doesn't work if there's only one of me?'

'That's right. Now if you had a wife to be Mother Wolf . . .'

'But I don't want a wife! I want a meal!' the wolf cried.

' . . .or a baby to be Little Wolf . . .'

'I've never liked cubs much. Noisy, rough little creatures. A baby would disturb my elegant bachelor life,' the wolf said.

'Then you can't expect me to be like Goldilocks and come in and eat your disgusting porridge and sit on your chairs and sleep in your dirty linen basket or your bath. Or even in a drawer,' Polly said.

'Is that your last word?' the wolf asked.

'Not quite. Don't read so many fairy stories, Wolf. Face real life instead. Whatever cunning plans you make to catch me and eat me, you are never going to succeed, because what you don't realize is that I'm Clever Polly and you are the . . .' But the wolf was looking so disappointed that Polly hadn't quite the heart to say what she really thought of his brains, so she ended her sentence ' . . . you are just a Unique Wolf.'

AT THE DOCTOR'S

When the wolf came into the doctor's waiting room, he saw that it was crowded. There were several old ladies and old gentlemen, who didn't interest him much. Too tough and stringy, he thought. But there were other patients who looked much more promising. One mother had two toddling twins, another had a succulent looking baby, and a fat little boy who was running round and round the table made the wolf's mouth water and his eyes glisten. He hoped that all the older people would get in to see the doctor first. Then, when he was left alone with the children, he would have a chance to seize one of them and leave quickly before anyone noticed.

'I don't have to go in to see the doctor today. I can always come back next week for what I need,' he thought.

The mother with the juicy baby was called next, but to the wolf's disappointment, she took the baby with her. Next, one of the old gentlemen left. The two old ladies went together. Then another old gentleman disappeared. Meanwhile, one of the twins had fallen asleep on a chair and, to the wolf's delight, its mother was the next to go into the surgery. She took the wakeful twin with her, but after a quick glance at the other, she left it sleeping.

The wolf got up and went over to the table. He pretended to be studying the books and magazines which covered it, picking one up one after another and turning the pages. Then he tucked one under his front leg and, as if by mistake, crossed the room so that he was sitting on the chair next to the sleeping twin.

The fat little boy who had been running round the room and falling over people's feet now stopped in front of the wolf.

'That's not your chair!' he said.

'It's not yours either,' the wolf said.

'You were sitting over there,' the fat little boy said, pointing.

'Yes, and now I'm sitting here,' the wolf said.

'Why?'

'So that I can look after this baby who's asleep,' the wolf said, seeing his chance.

'You aren't looking after it. Its Mum told my Mum to do that,' the little boy said.

'We can both look after it,' the wolf said.

'You don't look like someone who looks after babies.'

'Oh, but I am! I often look after babies. I'm very good at it. I look at them and wonder whether they'd be good to fry or . . . I mean, whether they're going to be good or if they're likely to cry. Things like that.'

'I don't believe . . . ' the little boy had begun to say, when his mother called him. 'Bill! Come over here! It's our turn to go and see the doctor. Hurry, now, or we'll miss our turn.'

'Aha! My chance has come,' the wolf thought, as he saw Bill and his mother leave the waiting room. He put out a paw towards the still sleeping twin, when its mother's arm came between them.

'It's all right, I'm back. Thank you so much for looking after her. It's difficult when you've got two at once, isn't it?' the twins' mother said, scooping up the spare twin, decanting it into a twin buggy which appeared from nowhere, and wheeling both babies briskly out of the waiting room.

Ten minutes later, the doctor's voice called, 'Mr Wolfe?' and the wolf reluctantly followed the white-coated figure along a passage to the surgery.

'Do sit down. New patient, I think. What seems to be the trouble?' the doctor asked, scribbling on a long white form in front of him.

'Trouble?' the wolf asked.

'WHAT DO YOU NOTICE WRONG?' the doctor said, very loudly and clearly.

'I'm not deaf!' the wolf said indignantly.

'I beg your pardon. I was asking you what seemed to be the trouble?' the doctor asked again.

The wolf did not know what to answer. Could he explain to this sympathetic doctor that the trouble was that he wanted to catch Polly and eat her? Or might this be misunderstood? He said, doubtfully, 'I have trouble with a girl. Quite a small one, but I can't seem to catch her when I want to.'

'A hyper-active child, perhaps?' the doctor asked.

'?'

'She is too active for you? Never sits still? Talks too quickly and too much?'

'Much too much,' the wolf agreed, glad to be understood at last.

'Sleeps badly?'

'I'm not sure about that.'

'Is she aggressive?'

'?'

'Aggressive. Fights with her mates. Won't do as she's told.'

'I don't know about her mates. She certainly never does what I tell her,' the wolf said.

'Argues a lot?'

'Never stops arguing. I can't tell you. Whatever I say or whatever I do, it's always talk, talk, argue, argue, till I don't know whether I'm standing on my head or my tail . . . my feet,' the wolf said.

'Is she in the waiting room? Let's have her in and I'll take a look at her,' the doctor said.

'No. You can't. She's not there. Anyway, what good would just looking at her do?' the wolf asked.

'Bring her in tomorrow, then. Anything else

bothering you?' the doctor asked, in the sort of voice that means, 'I haven't got time to listen to you any more, you'd better leave.'

'I'm bothered about not getting enough to eat. I'm hungry!' the wolf said, hoping that this would make the doctor more sympathetic.

The doctor looked more interested. 'Unnatural appetite?' he suggested.

'Depends on what you mean by unnatural. It's quite natural for a wo—— for the sort of person I am.'

'Three hearty meals a day, is that it?'

'When I get them,' the wolf said sadly.

'Good mixed diet? Plenty of veggies and fibre?'

'Veggies? Fibre?' The wolf shuddered.

'What, then? Convenience foods? Ready-made frozen stuff?'

'Meat,' the wolf said.

'Just meat? Nothing else at all? That's not what I call a healthy diet. Not to mention the expense.'

'I can eat cake. Polly once cooked a delicious cake,' the wolf remembered.

'Who is Polly? Never mind. What you need is an appetite depressant,' the doctor said, drawing his prescription pad towards him and beginning to scribble rapidly.

'A what?' the wolf asked, alarmed.

'Appetite depressant. Something to take the edge off your appetite so that you don't get these terrible feelings of hunger. And try to eat some fibre, there's nothing like it for filling the stomach. Good for the bowels too,' the doctor said.

'There's nothing wrong with my stomach. Or my bowels,' the wolf said, indignant.

'I'm surprised. Have this made up at the chemist, and come back and see me in a couple of weeks. And do, for goodness' sake try to get down some bran or wholemeal bread for breakfast. And, by the way, if you'd like to bring your little girl, I might be able to suggest a diet which will quieten her down a bit. Next please!' the doctor said briskly, opening his door and bustling the wolf out.

'Bran! What does he think I am, a rabbit? Whoever heard of a wolf eating bran?' the wolf asked himself as he walked down the street towards the chemist. While he was waiting for his prescription to be made up, he passed a tempting looking butchers and nipped in just in time to secure a large piece of steak for his supper. He

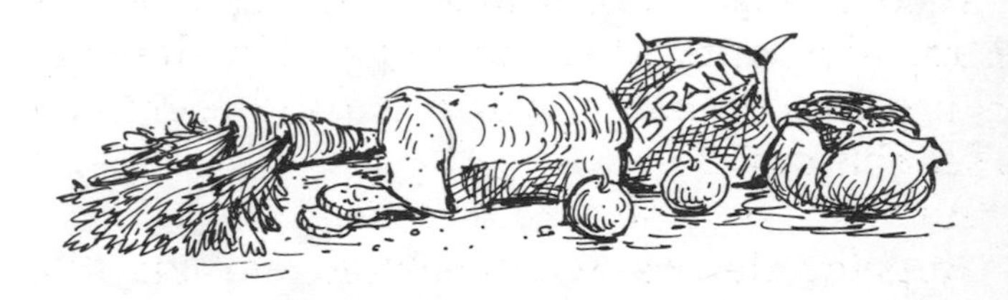

hadn't much faith in the doctor's advice for himself, but he decided that it would be worth while finding out what he might suggest to make Polly easier to catch.

It was nearly three weeks later that Polly saw the wolf waiting at the school gate at the end of the afternoon's lessons.

'Hi!' the wolf said as she came down the path.

'Hi, Wolf! What are you doing here?'

'Waiting for you,' the wolf said.

'I'm not going to walk home with you,' Polly said, remembering that there might not be many people about in the road where she lived.

'No, no. Of course not. That's not what I wanted to ask you.'

'What did you want to ask?'

'I wanted to tell you that I have consulted a very clever doctor.'

'Have you been ill? Poor Wolf!' Polly said, kindly.

'I have not been ill. I was consulting him about you.'

'But I haven't been ill either.'

'He says you are hyper-active.'

'No, I'm not! What's that mean, anyway?' Polly asked.

'Means you can't keep still and that you talk too much and argue too much and run about too

fast, and it isn't good for you.'

Polly began to understand what the wolf meant. She said, 'You mean I can run faster than you?'

'Only when I've just had dinner. Not now, this minute . . .'

'I'm not running. I'm staying here till my friends are ready to go home.'

'Ah. In that case . . . But no. I want to advise you about your diet.'

'You mean what I eat?'

'That's what diet means.'

'Go on, then. You can tell me, but I don't promise to do it.'

'This very clever doctor says you should cut out dairy foods.'

'What's that?'

'Milk. Cheese. Butter. Anything made with milk or cheese or butter. He says it will make you feel much better.'

'What about you, Wolf? Did he tell you what you should eat, too?'

'He was wrong,' the wolf said.

'What did he say?'

'He said . . . And I don't like bran and I hate vegetables.'

'What for? Why bran? Why vegetables?'

'To fill me up when I get hungry. Instead of . . .' The wolf stopped in the middle of his sentence. He did not mean to let Polly know that the doctor thought he ate too much meat. After all, what was Polly herself? Not bran. Certainly not a vegetable.

'Why didn't he tell you not to eat cheese and milk and all that?'

'I am not hyper-active,' the wolf said smugly.

'When he says hyper-whatever it is, he means clever,' Polly said.

'That's not what he said.'

'But he did say that talking and arguing a lot was hyper-something?'

'Ye-es.'

'Wouldn't you like to be clever, Wolf?'

'I am clever,' the wolf said.

'Clever-*er*, then? Cleverer than me?'

The wolf considered this. 'It might be an advantage, yes.'

'Then you ought to be eating all the things he said I shouldn't. Lots of butter and milk and cheese and cream. Then you'd always be able to run faster than me and you'd be cleverer than everyone else. That's sense, isn't it?'

The wolf thought about this for some time. It did seem sense. If those foods made Polly as quick and clever as she was, they ought to have the same effect on him.

'Why do you think the doctor told me to eat bran and vegetables, then?' he asked.

'Perhaps he guessed that you wanted to catch me to eat and he didn't like the idea,' Polly said.

'But that's unfair! It was me went to see him and asked for his advice! He ought to have been on my side!' the wolf cried.

'People are unfair,' Polly said, with feeling.

'He cheated me!'

'But anyway, now you know what to do,' Polly said.

'I'm going straight off to the dairy. I'm going to drink a pint of double cream and eat as much cheese as I can swallow. And next time we meet,

Stupid little Polly, you'll see, I shall run like the wind and my brain will be working so well it will dazzle you. As for you, you'd better go on my diet. Cabbages and bran. We shall meet again,' the wolf cried as he left the school gate and walked sedately down the road. Polly looked after him. Oh Wolf! You certainly aren't dazzling me with your cleverness yet, she thought.

IN SHEEP'S CLOTHING

The wolf stood in the school playground, waiting for the children to come out at the end of the afternoon. The parents, mostly mothers, who were waiting there too, looked at him suspiciously and none of them came over to speak to him. He was so very dark, so very hairy. None of them could remember noticing him there before.

Boys and girls began straggling out of the building. Some clutched large sheets of paper on which they had painted portraits of their families. Others carried egg-boxes, cardboard cylinders from used toilet rolls, empty cotton reels, shells, nuts, melon seeds and corks, from which they had made pretty and possibly useful gifts. For Christmas was coming, and the children in this school were encouraged to be generous with their time and ingenuity.

The wolf had to wait for what seemed a long time before he saw Polly in a group of children,

talking excitedly. This lot carried something different. One child had a pair of large wings in her hand, two more had long, striped robes over their arms, and Polly was carrying a baby doll wrapped in a long white shawl.

'Hi, Wolf!' Polly called out when she saw him.

'Hi, Polly! What's that doll for? I thought you didn't play with dolls.'

'I don't. Not much. Anyway this doll isn't mine, she's Lucy's. I just borrowed her for the nativity play.'

'What sort of play?' the wolf asked.

'A nativity play.'

'What's that?'

'It's about the first Christmas. You know. Jesus being born in a stable and all that. We're acting it the day after tomorrow, and I'm going to be

Mary. She's Jesus' mother. It's the best part.'

'A play! Couldn't I be in it too?' he said. Surely acting in a play with Polly and several other deliciously small children would give him a chance to get one of them.

'It's only for my class to act in. And there aren't any more parts to go round.'

'Who else is there besides Mary and that doll?'

'There's Joseph. Benjie is being Joseph. And there're some angels. Sophie over there is an angel. You can see her wings.'

'Why isn't she wearing them on her back if she's an angel?'

'She will when we act our play. There's an

innkeeper, that's Michael. He has to say, "No room, no room." And then we go into the stable and I have the baby.'

'Anyone else?' the wolf asked.

'Three kings . . .'

'Couldn't I be a king? I'd be very good as a king,' the wolf suggested, rather fancying himself in a crown.

'No, you couldn't. Derek's one of them and the twins are being the other two. And Marmaduke's being King Herod, who's horrible and wants to kill all the babies.'

'To eat?' the wolf asked.

'I don't think so. And there are a lot of shepherds. They don't have much to say, so they're the children in my class who can't remember long speeches.'

The wolf had brightened at the sound of shepherds. 'Shepherds? With sheep?'

'I suppose so. But no one wants to act a sheep.'

'I would,' the wolf said.

'You? Be a sheep? But you're nothing like a sheep.'

'I could act like a sheep.'

Polly wasn't sure that he could. 'How?' she asked.

'Baaa. Baaa . . . aa. Baa . . . a . . . baa . . . a. Baa!' the wolf said loudly. Several of the parents standing in the playground turned round to look and one or two of them laughed.

'How was that?' the wolf said, pleased with the effect.

'It wasn't bad. But you don't look like a sheep.'

'I haven't dressed for the part yet. After all, when I came out this afternoon, I had no idea I might be asked to be in a play.'

'No one has asked you,' Polly said.

'So when is the performance, Polly?' the wolf went on, taking no notice of this remark.

'The day after tomorrow. Wolf . . .!' Polly began, but before she could finish the sentence, the wolf had gone. 'Benjie. Sophie. Marmaduke. Not to mention Polly. And a lot of shepherds who are too stupid to say anything. I ought to get one of them,' he thought as he trotted home.

When he got there, he went straight to his larder; this was something he always did, sometimes hoping that though he had left it nearly empty when he went out, it might miraculously have filled up in his absence. But the shelves were as bare as before. The wolf sighed, shut the larder door and walked into his sitting room where, on the floor, lay a not very clean, whitish-grey fur rug. It had belonged to the wolf's grandfather, and how he had got it it is probably better not to know. It was, in fact, a whole sheepskin, and it was the thought of this priceless possession that had made the wolf so confident that he could take part in Polly's nativity play.

For the rest of that day and for most of the next, the wolf practised. He practised with pieces of string and with safety pins and elastic bands. He even tried to sew with a needle and thread. For most of the time, he practised in front of his long mirror, and at last, on the very morning of the performance, he was satisfied. He not only sounded like a sheep, he now looked like one. After a light midday meal, he carefully dressed himself in his disguise and made his way to Polly's school, using side streets so as to avoid notice.

He managed to slink in at a back door. He heard a gabble of excited voices coming from a

classroom further along the passage and, looking cautiously through a glass door, he saw a great many children dressed for the play. He saw a couple of angels in long white nightgowns and gauzy wings. He saw two kings, exactly like each other, wearing golden crowns. He saw several boys and girls in striped robes, with pieces of material wound round their heads. One of them carried a small stuffed lamb under his arm. So these were the shepherds, the wolf guessed. On the further side of the classroom, he saw Polly in a blue dress, with a blue veil on her head, holding the doll baby by one leg, upside down.

The wolf pushed the door open and joined the actors.

'Hey! Who're you pushing?' angrily asked a small stout king in a red robe edged with gold tinsel.

The wolf swallowed a snarl and the temptation to take a mouthful out of a plump leg very near to him, and said, 'I just want to get over to the shepherds.' He knew he would have to be careful until everyone was off their guard and thinking about nothing but the play. He did not want to make a disturbance, and he was particularly anxious that Polly should not see him yet.

'Timmy! here's one of your sheep!' the red king shouted.

'We haven't got any sheep,' a shepherd called back.

'There's one here. Don't know who. Miss Wright must've got someone in extra.'

Lucky, thought the wolf, that no one seemed surprised at this, and no one took any particular interest in him. He lay down under one of the tables pushed against the wall and amused himself by remarking which children were fatter or slower (or both) and so would be the easiest prey. After a short time he noticed that the teacher was looking over each child's costume, hitching up the wings on one angel, tying up Joseph's shoelaces (they came undone again a moment later) and taking the doll baby away from Polly–Mary. 'You don't have the baby in the first scene, that's when the angel comes to tell you you're going to have it,' she said, and put in on a chair.

'Now, we're all going into the hall. Very, very quiet, please. Sophie and Polly, are you ready for Scene One? The others can stand at the side and watch, but no talking and no fighting. Understand?' She gave the three kings a special glare, and led the way out of the classroom.

The wolf trotted quietly behind the children. Along one long passage, turn a corner, another passage, and then a swing door into the hall. People were singing. The wolf caught one or two words: ' . . . midwinter . . . snow . . . snow . . . long ago.' It sounded cold and disagreeable.

Why not sing about something pleasant, like hot soup, a roast joint? chips? He found himself jostled among the children and crowded into a small space at the side of the stage, with one of the kings leaning against his shoulder and a shepherd treading on a hind paw. 'I wish . . .' So many juicy little arms and legs all round him. 'But I must wait. If I gave myself away now, I'd never get out of here alive,' he thought, and licked his chops silently.

The singing had stopped. The curtain was drawn back from the front of the stage, and the wolf heard, 'Hi, Mary. You're going to have a baby and it's called Jesus.'

'But I'm not even married!' Polly's voice answered.

'That doesn't matter, because it's God's baby,' the angel said and walked off. Then Joseph walked on and told Mary they had got to go on a long journey. 'But I'm going to have a baby!' Mary said, and Joseph said, never mind that, she could have the baby in a hotel somewhere on the way.

'When do we get to the shepherds?' the wolf asked a child next to him in a loud whisper. He was bored with all this talk about the baby.

'Not till after the baby's got born, silly,' the child whispered back.

'No talking!' Miss Wright's voice hissed behind them, and the wolf had to wait while

Mary and Joseph were told that there was no room in the inn. 'But you can use the stable, if you like,' the innkeeper said kindly.

There was some more singing. The wolf was by now not only squashed, but also terribly hot. The children round him were all warm and excited and he was wearing an extra skin. An elastic band round one of his ankles was too tight, and a shepherd behind him was apt to tread on the fleshy part of his tail. It was a relief when Miss Thompson whispered, 'Go on, Timmy, it's the shepherds now,' and the group round the wolf moved out on to the stage.

The lights were bright here, and for a minute the wolf's eyes were dazzled. Then he saw Polly, in her blue veil, sitting on a stool, surrounded by bales of straw, with the doll baby on her lap. Joseph stood behind her. The shepherds moved towards her and the wolf followed them.

'Hullo, Mary. We heard about your baby, so we've come to have a look at him,' the largest shepherd said.

'You're welcome,' Polly said. She still hadn't seen the wolf.

'We've brought him some presents. Here's an apple,' one of the younger shepherds said, holding out the apple.

'Thank you. I'm sure he likes apples,' Polly said.

'And I've brought a lamb,' another shepherd said.

The wolf thought this was a good moment to give a loud Baa . . . a . . . a. Everyone jumped, and the child carrying the stuffed toy lamb said, 'You aren't supposed to say that.'

'Why not? I'm a sheep, aren't I? "Baa" is sheep language,' the wolf said.

'You didn't say that when we rehearsed yesterday,' the first shepherd said.

'I wasn't here yesterday. But I am today. Baa . . . . aa,' the wolf said, annoyed.

'He's made me forget what I was supposed to

say,' the smallest shepherd said, and burst into tears.

'It doesn't matter, just go on. Thank you for the lamb, it will be nice for Jesus to play with when he's older,' Polly said, quickly.

'You're not the lamb I'm giving Jesus, this is,' said Timmy, showing the toy lamb.

'I don't think he's a lamb at all. He's got black paws,' another shepherd said.

'Some sheep do have black feet. And black noses,' the wolf said.

'He's got a long black tail that sticks out behind, too,' the second shepherd said.

'I haven't! Have I?' The wolf tried to look over his shoulder. There was a tearing sound and the wolf was aware that the fleece was slipping badly and a large safety pin at the back of his neck had come open.

'I don't think he's a sheep either,' Joseph said, interested, and coming round to look.

'I'm not! I'm a wo——' the wolf began, but Polly interrupted. 'Of course he's a sheep. He came in with the shepherds, didn't he? And he's wearing a sheep's coat.'

'Polly, you know who I am. Tell them,' the wolf complained.

'Children, get on with the play, it's time you made room for the kings,' Miss Wright hissed from the side of the stage.

'I expect you want to get back to watch your flocks by night,' Polly said politely to the shepherds, who began to shuffle towards the way out. To the wolf she whispered, 'You stay here. And don't forget, you chose to be a sheep in this play, now you've got to act like one.'

'You mean I've got to go on saying "Baa"?'

'That's right. Just "Baa" and nothing else.'

'Don't I get anything to eat?'

'Sheep eat grass. I don't think there is any grass round here. There's a little straw if you'd like that.'

'Don't sheep eat meat ever? Not a mouthful of leg?' the wolf asked, gazing at the fat little leg of one of the three kings who were now preparing to offer their gifts to the baby Jesus.

'Certainly not! Thank you very much, that'll make a nice smell in this stable,' Polly said to the third king, who had just given her a box supposed to contain myrrh.

'But I'm not an ordinary sheep. And I'm hungry!' the wolf said, rather too loud. The fat-legged king turned round and said, 'SShh! It's my turn to talk now. We're going home without seeing Harold again because we know he means to try to kill your baby. That's all. Bye-bye.'

'Who's Harold?' the wolf asked, wondering whether this was someone who shared his taste in food.

'Herod, not Harold. Don't talk, Wolf. You're not supposed to say anything but "Baa".'

'But that's silly.'

'Sheep are silly. If you wanted to do something clever, Wolf, you ought to have acted a different part.'

'So I've got to go on being a silly sheep and I can't catch anyone? Not even you?'

'I'm afraid so. I'm sorry, Wolf. Joseph and I have got to go now. But you can stay for a bit and go on being a sheep, if you want to. Until we've all gone home, then you can go back to being a stup—— to being a wolf again. Come on Joseph, it's time we went to Egypt,' said Clever Polly, and left.

YOU HAVE TO SUFFER IN ORDER TO BE BEAUTIFUL

The wolf stood in front of his long mirror and looked at himself all over.

'Nothing wrong there. Long legs, lean, healthy body, kind, intelligent face. No two ways about it, I'm a good-looking fellow,' he thought. He pulled in his stomach and bent a front leg to make the muscles stand out. 'And I'm not really overweight. I've got big bones, that's all.'

'I've been making a mistake. I shouldn't have told Polly that what I really want is to eat her. I should have pretended that I admired her. In stories, the girl always falls for the man who says he wants to marry her . . . Ugh!' The wolf shook his head. 'Why are they always so keen on marriage? But if I pretended to want to marry Polly, then when I'd got her home with me . . . Yes, that's it! I shall woo her. After all, it wasn't always handsome young princes those girls fell for. Look at Beauty and the Bea——. Well, Polly isn't exactly Beauty, so she can't expect to get a Prince.'

'Yes, Mr Woolf. And may I ask how you came to hear of me?' the immensely smooth, pink-cheeked doctor asked the wolf, who was sitting on the opposite side of an elegant desk in a consulting room in a private health clinic.

'I saw your advertisement . . .'

'I never advertise. It is not allowed in medical practice,' the doctor said, displeased.

'I read something in the newspaper that said you could work miracles. Make people look different.'

'Perhaps miracles is a slight exaggeration. But certainly many of my clients tell me that they are very happy with what I am able to do for them. So what can I do for you?' the doctor asked.

'It's a very delicate matter,' the wolf said.

'Ah! Perhaps you have some special reason for coming to see me at this moment of time?' the doctor suggested.

'Yes, I have. A very special reason.' Because if I look quite different, and Polly doesn't recognize me, I'll have a better chance of catching her, had been the wolf's clever idea.

'An affair of the heart, perhaps? There is some girl you wish to approach? But so far, you have not dared?'

'I can dare, all right. But she won't listen to me.'

'You wanted to make some changes to your

appearance?' the doctor asked.

'What sort of thing do you suggest?' the wolf asked.

'Well, for instance, noses. Not everyone is satisfied with the nose they have. I can alter a nose to almost anything you might require. Roman? Snub? Classical? Short and appealing? Long and learned? Now in your case, Mr Woolf, I should suggest a certain curtailing . . .'

'Doing what? My tail's all right,' the wolf exclaimed in alarm.

'Curtailing. Shortening. It has no effect on the olfactory function, I assure you?'

'Olfactory?' the wolf asked.

'You'll be able to smell with it as well as before.'

'So I should hope! If I couldn't smell, I might just as well not have a nose,' the wolf said.

'Then there are teeth. I work in conjunction with a first-class dental surgeon. Now it seems to me that your teeth leave quite a lot to be desired. If you'll forgive my saying so, they are on the large side and a little discoloured. It happens in later life, you know.'

'Later life! I'm in my prime!' the wolf said, angrily.

'Of course. I did not mean to imply . . . But you might like to consider a really good set of dentures. Something smaller and whiter. I assure you, it would have a really dramatic effect on your general appearance.'

'Dentures? What are dentures?' the wolf asked.

'New teeth. Fitting perfectly so that there would never be any danger of them slipping and so causing you unnecessary embarrassment,' the doctor said.

'You mean false teeth?'

'Exactly. Dentures.'

'Would they be able to gnaw bones?'

'Certainly.'

'And chew up a juicy little gir——, a juicy little Pol——, juicy little anything?'

'They would function perfectly,' the doctor said.

'He's awfully difficult to understand. It must be being so clever makes him use all these long words,' the wolf thought. Aloud he said, 'I'm not sure about false teeth. I'll think about it.'

The doctor looked him over carefully. 'Then, if you don't mind my suggesting it, we might tackle the problem of superfluous hair.'

'What's that?' the wolf asked, puzzled again.

'Superfluous hair. You are more bountifully endowed with hair than most of us.' The doctor himself, indeed, was almost completely bald. 'We could tackle that with electrolysis, though I must warn you that it would take time.'

'What do you want to do with my hair?' the wolf asked, not having understood a word of this last sentence.

'Remove it. Not all of it, of course. Just some around the upper part of the face, to give you a more open, friendly expression.'

'I've got a friendly expression,' the wolf said.

'Of course, Mr Woolf. Delightful expression. But a *leetle* difficult to see with that very luxuriant growth of hair over the forehead and cheeks. I can't help feeling that this young woman you are interested in might respond to – shall we say, a less hirsute approach.'

'Her suit? Or my suit? But I haven't got one!' the wolf cried, thoroughly confused by all this language.

'She might like you better without so much hair,' the doctor said, annoyed at having to use ordinary words.

'What was that word you used about my hair?' the wolf asked.

'Superfluous. Means you have too much of it,' the doctor said.

'Not that one. Electro something.'

'Electrolysis. It is a means of eliminating super—— unwanted hair, by the insertion of an electric needle into each hair root . . .'

'Sounds uncomfortable. Does it hurt?' the wolf asked.

'Only for a moment,' the doctor assured him.

'And that gets rid of the lot? All in a moment?'

'No, no, Mr Woolf. Each individual hair has to be dealt with separately.'

'Wow! And these extra teeth? I suppose it doesn't hurt to have another set to put in when you need them?'

'Having first extracted the original dentition.'

'?' said the wolf.

'First of all, we take out everything you've got there.'

The wolf shuddered.

'What about the nose job?'

'That necessitates a few days in hospital while we break down the bones of your face and construct a totally new form. Sometimes we have to take a little skin from a leg or arm in order to cover the new nasal apparatus.'

'Take skin from whose leg or arm?'

'Yours, of course, Mr Woolf. It is a perfectly simple procedure.'

'I'll think about it,' the wolf said. He did not mean to think about it at all. He saw that all these operations were going to hurt a lot, and he did not mean to suffer that much even in order to catch stupid little Polly.

'My secretary will see you on your way out,' the doctor said, rising from his chair and shaking the wolf's paw rather coolly. He did not believe that this client was likely to come back to ask for a complete reconstruction of his appearance, however much he wanted to get his girl.

'That will be one hundred and fifty pounds, Mr Woolf,' the charming secretary said, as the wolf passed through her office.

'A hundred and fifty? Pounds? You must be joking!' the wolf snorted.

'Will it be cash or a cheque?' the charming secretary asked.

'I haven't got my cheque book on me just

now,' the wolf said. This was not surprising, as he did not have a cheque book anywhere.

'Perhaps you could drop a cheque in the post this afternoon?' the secretary said.

'Perhaps,' the wolf said, and left. 'A hundred and fifty pounds, for threatening to break the bones in my face, skin my leg, take out all my teeth and electrocute my fur? The man's a monster!' the wolf thought as he hurried down the street.

'Polly,' the wolf said, looking over the fence into Polly's front garden, where she was lazily swinging herself in the sun.

'Yes, Wolf?'

'Would you like me better if I didn't have so much hair . . . fur?'

'Bald all over, d'you mean? No, I wouldn't. I think you'd look terrible,' Polly said.

'Suppose I had an extra lot of teeth? False ones?'

'What for? You've got enough, haven't you?'

'Or if I had my nose shaped differently?'

'But you wouldn't look like a wolf if you had a different nose,' Polly said.

'But would you like me any better?'

'No. I like you just as you are,' Polly said, quite affectionately.

'Wonderful! Then come with me, Polly. Now!

To my home. Make me the happiest of . . . wolves.'

Polly laughed. 'No, thank you, Wolf. I like you a lot, but I don't trust you for a minute. I like you where you are now – on the other side of the garden fence. And like a wolf, not with your long nose made short or with all your teeth pulled out. Just go on being yourself, and I'll stay like I am. Safe,' said Clever Polly.

KIND POLLY AND THE WOLF IN DANGER

This story is different from all the other stories about Polly and the wolf, because it doesn't start with the wolf planning how he can have Polly to eat.

One day, Polly went out to do some shopping for her mother in the village. She had bought a cauliflower and some potatoes at the vegetable shop, and a pound of sugar and half a pound of biscuits at the grocer's, and she was thinking of going home again, when she heard a loud noise coming from a side street. She ran to the corner and looked along the street and saw a crowd of people all very angry about something. The people were shouting and someone was howling. Polly thought that she knew that howl, and she hurried up the street.

As she got nearer the crowd, she could hear more distinctly what the people were saying.

'Ought not to be allowed!'

'Would worry the sheep!'

'Cause a dog fight!'

'Steal a hen!'

'These beasts are dangerous. Should be behind bars!'

'Might bite a baby!'

'Could easily kill a child!'

'Someone muzzle it!'

'Someone shoot it!'

Polly began to believe that she knew whom the voices were talking about, but she still hadn't managed to get through the crowd to see if she had guessed right. Now she heard other voices saying other things.

'Interesting shape. Don't know if I've ever seen one exactly like that before. A new breed, perhaps?'

'Look it up in the *Gazette*.'

'Like to have a look at its bones. Preserve the skeleton in formaldehyde . . .'

'Curious sound it makes. Don't know if I've ever heard a dog howl exactly like that . . .'

Polly pushed through the inner ring of trousers and skirts and saw a wooden tea chest set up on end. Out of the top of the tea chest stuck the head of the wolf, and over this head, someone had thrown a net, which was held down by the edges of the chest. The wolf was in a bad way. His fur was draggled, he was trembling and he was looking this way and that with huge, terrified eyes.

'It'd make a splendid exhibit for the local museum. Stuffed, of course,' a large man in a tweed jacket was saying. Polly saw a glimmer of hope cross the wolf's face, and she realized that he was thinking of being stuffed as an agreeable sensation after a large meal. But the hope disappeared the next moment, as a woman added, 'You have to be careful how you kill an animal you want to stuff. A bullet through the heart is fine, but whoever shoots must know how to be accurate.'

'I'm against killing. This animal should be in a zoo,' another woman said.

'Doesn't look in very good shape to me. Death might be a mercy,' a man said.

'Shouldn't be shot, though. Call in the local vet.'

'Spoilsport! Why not have a chase? We could get the hounds. Creature would enjoy a good run for its money,' said another voice.

'Cruel! I object! No blood sports here!' said someone else.

'In any case its body should be preserved for expert examination.'

'Call the police!'

'Send for the Master of the Hunt!'

'Fetch my gun!'

The voices grew louder and more quarrelsome. Everyone seemed to be shouting at everyone else.

Polly managed to edge closer. 'Wolf!' she said.

The wolf turned his miserable eyes towards her.

'You here?' he said.

'What happened? Why are they all so angry? What did you do?'

'I didn't do anything,' the wolf said, sullenly.

'I don't believe that. Tell me the truth.'

'I didn't do anything out of the ordinary. I've seen plenty of people do it.'

'Go on.'

'I've often seen people go round sniffing at other people's babies.'

'Sniffing at them?' Polly asked, surprised.

'Bending right over their prams, with their noses in the children's faces. And you can hear them smacking their lips.'

'Probably kissing them.'

'Nonsense! Sniffing to see if they're ready to eat. Smacking their lips when they know what a good meal they're going to have.'

'Is that what you did?' Polly asked.

'Only one or two. The first was a scrawny little thing, not worth its salt. The second wasn't any good, either. It hit me. I did not hit back. Naturally I didn't want a struggle.'

'And then?'

'Then I saw exactly what I needed. Small, plump, juicy-looking. Not unlike you, a few years ago. I was just unwrapping it, to make sure it was perfectly fresh, when this woman came dashing out of the shop and started screeching and calling me all sorts of names, and then a

couple of men came up and got hold of my legs, and they held my jaws so that I couldn't speak, and they pushed me into this revolting box and covered me with a net.'

'Oh Wolf! What did you expect? Had you forgotten that people don't eat babies?'

'I can't think why not. There seems to be a very good supply,' the wolf said.

'Would you eat wolf cubs?'

'Certainly. If I was hungry.'

'Well, most people don't eat babies. So when they saw you sniffing into prams, they realized that you weren't a human. They knew you were a wolf.'

'No, they don't. They don't know what I am. Didn't you hear what they said? They think I'm very unusual,' wolf said, with a little pride.

'Don't be too pleased about that. It's because you're so unusual that they want to dissect you.'

'What's dissect?' the wolf asked.

'Cut you up to find out how you work.'

'Cut me up alive!' the wolf cried.

'Not alive. Dead.'

'Cut me up, dead?'

'Or shoot you and stuff you. Not with food. With cotton wool, or whatever you stuff dead creatures with,' Polly explained.

The wolf shuddered.

'Or they might want to hunt you. With dogs.'

'What am I going to do?' the wolf said, and at his howl, several people in the crowd turned round to see what was happening.

'Don't stand so close, little girl. That animal is dangerous,' a man in spectacles said.

'I've met him before,' Polly said.

'Then you know that he is a threat to our community,' Spectacles said.

Polly thought quickly. 'I'll tell you what I do know. He's a very strange animal. There's never been anything quite like him here before.' (That's true enough, she said to herself.) 'In fact he's Unique.'

'I am NOT,' she heard the wolf mutter behind the net, but she took no notice and went on.

'You know what a fuss everyone makes about not letting rare kinds of plants and animals disappear. I can tell you, if you hurt this animal, there's going to be a terrible fuss. You'll get blamed by everyone important. The Queen will be angry, and the Prime Minister will be furious, and I wouldn't wonder if the whole village didn't get punished.'

There were murmurs among the crowd. They were obviously impressed. She heard, 'Seems to know what she's talking about.' 'Don't want the place to get a bad name.' 'Remember what the Green Party said on television the other night, about preserving the balance of Nature.'

'I expect one of the television stars would tell everyone what a terrible thing had happened here,' Polly said, reminded of the power of TV.

'She's right. We don't want to be held up to scorn as vandals,' the tweedy man said.

'Animal Rights,' said a thin woman who hadn't spoken before.

'I still think it should be put behind bars. In a zoo,' said a fat man.

'Polly! I won't go into a zoo,' the wolf said in an undertone.

'Can't I have it to keep in my room?' a small boy asked his mum, who said, 'Sorry, sweetie, I don't think Dad would like it.'

'That wouldn't be too bad,' the wolf said, looking over the small boy hungrily.

'He shouldn't be in a zoo. He should be allowed to roam free,' Polly said.

'Not around our village!' someone said quickly.

'Where he belongs. In forests, or on hills.

Wherever he came from,' the thin woman said.

'Where did you come from, Wolf?' Polly asked, wondering why she had never asked this question before.

'Can't remember. I didn't come out of a box, I do know that.'

'In fact, he's almost certainly one of an endangered species,' Polly said.

'I don't! I wouldn't, anyway, if you let me go!' the wolf cried.

'Wouldn't what?' Polly asked.

'Make dangerous speeches. It's not the sort of thing I do.'

'I didn't say speeches, I said . . . what that means is that you're very special and we ought to take great care nothing terrible happens to you.'

'Now that makes sense . . . Why don't all the other . . . ' the wolf began, but he was interrupted by the man in spectacles, who had raised his hand and said, 'Ahem! Ahem! It seems to me that we should take a vote on the question of what to do with this . . . this . . . unusual animal. I for one am not prepared to take the responsibility of advising its destruction . . .'

'What's that?' the wolf whispered to Polly.

'Killing you,' Polly whispered back.

' . . . by whatever means. The choice therefore lies between sending it to one of the many zoological institutions in this country, or, as my friend here has suggested, letting it go free to its natural habitat . . .'

'Natural what?' the wolf wanted to know.

'Where you live, Wolf.'

' . . . wherever that may be. Could we have a show of hands, please? Those wishing the animal to go to a zoo put up their hands.'

He counted. 'Four . . . six . . . Are you holding up your hand, Madam, or adjusting a hatpin? . . . Seven . . .'

'Wolf! If I loosened the net here, could you creep out?' Polly whispered. She had discovered that she could pull the edge of the net a little away from the bottom of the tea chest.

'If I make myself very thin.'

'And if I do, will you promise . . .?' But Spectacles had now finished the first count and there were too many people looking round. Polly waited till she heard the second counting begin. Then she finished the sentence. 'Will you promise not to try to catch me to eat ever again?'

'Of course. I promise. Now let me out,' the Wolf said, far too quickly.

'You didn't mean that. Think about it.'

The wolf thought. 'You mean really, truly, never?'

'Really, truly, never.'

'But it's been fun! Hasn't it?'

'Sometimes. Frightening, too.'

'Being frightened is fun. And anyway, you're so clever, Polly. You've always managed to escape up till now.'

'You've never said I was clever before,' Polly said.

'I didn't realize how clever you are till I heard you say that about dangerous speeches,' the wolf said.

Polly was pleased. She began to say, 'Well, just promise . . .' But the sentence never got said, for at that moment the wolf, seeing that she wasn't thinking about holding the net as tightly as before, pushed his head up and pulled it out of her hands. There was a bump, a crash, and a moment later, the wolf was out of the tea chest, free of the net, and was streaking down the High Street, terrifying passers-by and only just avoiding cars and bicycles.

Luckily no one blamed Polly. 'But I wonder what he thinks his natural habitat is? I'm sure it's not forests or hills, it's much more likely to be this village where he knows his way around,' she thought and wondered if she would ever see him again. Probably. He wasn't likely to give up now that on this occasion it had been the wolf who had flattered and fooled her. Clever Polly had for once met a not so stupid wolf.